A Note to Parents and Caregivers:

Read-it! Readers are for children who are just starting on the amazing road to reading. These beautiful books support both the acquisition of reading skills and the love of books.

The PURPLE LEVEL presents basic topics and objects using high frequency words and simple language patterns.

The RED LEVEL presents familiar topics using common words and repeating sentence patterns.

The BLUE LEVEL presents new ideas using a larger vocabulary and varied sentence structure.

The YELLOW LEVEL presents more challenging ideas, a broad vocabulary, and wide variety in sentence structure.

The GREEN LEVEL presents more complex ideas, an extended vocabulary range, and expanded language structures.

The ORANGE LEVEL presents a wide range of ideas and concepts using challenging vocabulary and complex language structures.

When sharing a book with your child, read in short stretches, pausing often to talk about the pictures. Have your child turn the pages and point to the pictures and familiar words. And be sure to reread favorite stories or parts of stories.

There is no right or wrong way to share books with children. Find time to read with your child, and pass on the legacy of literacy.

Adria F. Klein, Ph.D.
Professor Emeritus
California State University
San Bernardino, California

For my good friend Julie, even though she likes cats—J.K.

Editor: Christianne Jones
Designer: Amy Muehlenhardt
Page Production: Lori Bye
Art Director: Nathan Gassman
The illustrations in this book were created with watercolor and pen.

Picture Window Books
5115 Excelsior Boulevard
Suite 232
Minneapolis, MN 55416
877-845-8392
www.picturewindowbooks.com

Printed in the United States of America.

Library of Congress Cataloging-in-Publication Data
Kalz, Jill.
Tuckerbean at Waggle World / by Jill Kalz ; illustrated by Benton Mahan.
p. cm. — (Read-it! readers)
Summary: While at Waggle World, an amusement park for pets and their owners,
Tuckerbean experiences the delights and terrors of a fun house when he wanders
away from his master, Peni.
ISBN-13: 978-1-4048-3388-3 (library binding)
ISBN-10: 1-4048-3388-9 (library binding)
ISBN-13: 978-1-4048-3389-0 (paperback)
ISBN-10: 1-4048-3389-7 (paperback)
[1. Dogs—Fiction. 2. Pets—Fiction. 3. Amusement parks—Fiction. 4. Lost and
found possessions—Fiction.] I. Mahan, Ben, ill. II. Title.
PZ7.K12655Tuck 2006
[E]—dc22   2006027302

Tuckerbean at Waggle World

by Jill Kalz
illustrated by Benton Mahan

Special thanks to our advisers for their expertise:

Adria F. Klein, Ph.D.
Professor Emeritus, California State University
San Bernardino, California

Susan Kesselring, M.A.
Literacy Educator
Rosemount–Apple Valley–Eagan (Minnesota) School District

PiCTURE WiNDOW BOOKS
Minneapolis, Minnesota

Peni couldn't sit still. She had a secret.

"Keep your eyes closed, Tuckerbean," she said.
"Don't peek!"

When Peni's mom opened the door,
Tuckerbean kept his eyes closed.

When Peni clicked his seat belt, he kept his eyes closed. But when she giggled, he peeked.

Flags flapped high in the air. Flowers bloomed everywhere. Two giant dogs held a big sign.

Tuckerbean was at Waggle World!

Peni and Tuckerbean ran into the park. They saw big dogs, small dogs, and long dogs.

They saw dogs with curly hair, straight hair, and no hair! Some dogs woofed. Others yipped and yapped.

Peni and Tuckerbean rode the ferris wheel.

They rode the ponies around and around.

They bumped each other in the bumper cars.

They rode the roller coaster up and down.

Tuckerbean couldn't go on the next ride with Peni. He wasn't tall enough.

"Wait here, Tuckerbean. I'll be back soon,"
Peni said.

But Tuckerbean didn't wait. He went exploring.

At the fun house, lights flashed, and horns honked. Laughter filled the air.

Squirrels dressed like clowns whistled and spun.

One room was full of mirrors. In the first mirror, Tuckerbean looked tall and skinny. In the second mirror, he looked short and fat.

In the third mirror, his head looked as big as a beach ball. In the fourth mirror, it looked as small as a marble.

When Tuckerbean turned around, he saw four Tuckerbeans!

Each one had fluffy white hair and a big black nose.

Suddenly, Tuckerbean saw four monsters with purple polka dots standing behind him!

Each one had a long snout and large, pointy teeth.

Tuckerbean closed his eyes. He kept them closed tight.

But when he heard Peni giggle, he peeked.

"We looked all over for you, silly bean!" Peni exclaimed. "Promise us you won't wander away again, OK?"

Tuckerbean wagged his tail and barked. Then Peni, her mom, and Tuckerbean ran down the path toward the snow cone stand. After the exciting day, it was time for a treat!

More *Read-it!* Readers

Bright pictures and fun stories help you practice your reading skills. Look for more books at your level.

Looking for a specific title or level? A complete list of *Read-it!* Readers is available on our Web site:

www.picturewindowbooks.com